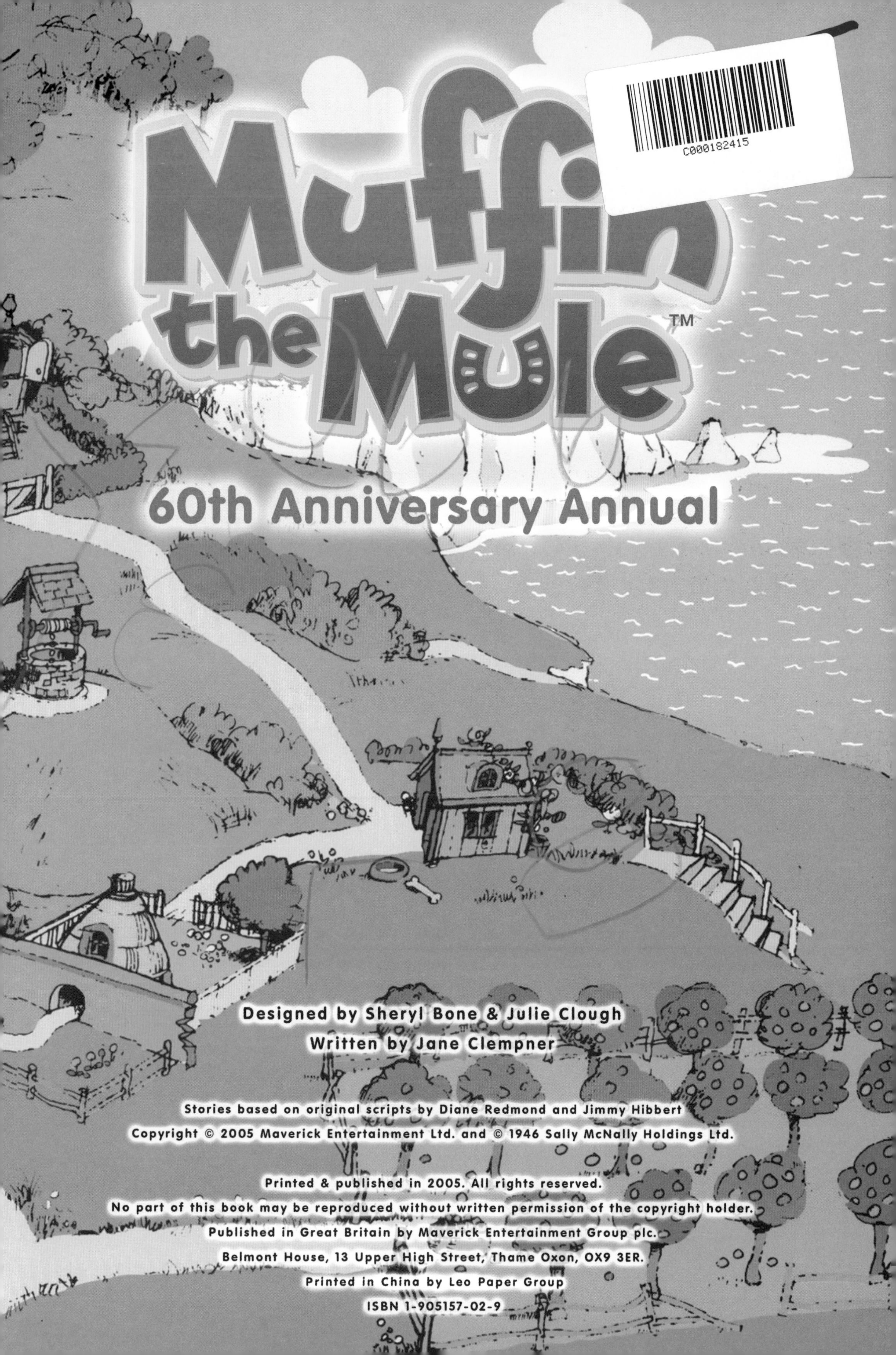

Muffin the Mule™

60th Anniversary Annual

Designed by Sheryl Bone & Julie Clough
Written by Jane Clempner

Stories based on original scripts by Diane Redmond and Jimmy Hibbert

Published in Great Britain by Maverick Entertainment Group plc.
Belmont House, 13 Upper High Street, Thame Oxon, OX9 3ER.
Printed in China by Leo Paper Group
ISBN 1-905157-02-9

Annual

My name is 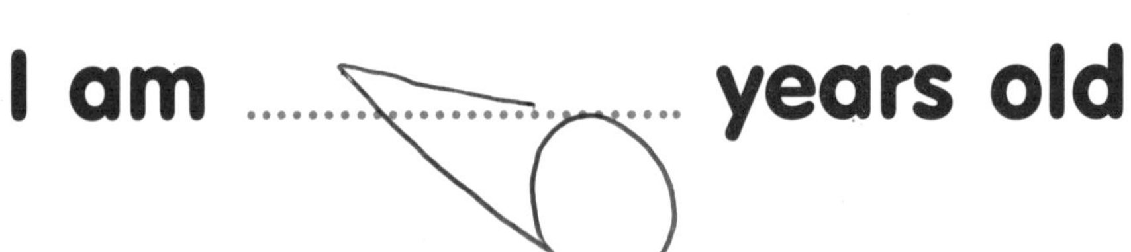 ....

I am .... years old

I live in ....

Look out for us in the annual!

When you see me, it's Time to think!

When you see me, it's Time to draw!

When you see me, it's Time to colour!

Contents

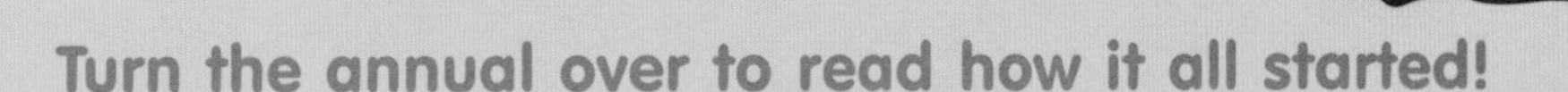

Turn the annual over to read how it all started!

Hello!
Welcome to Muffinham.
I'd love to take you on some adventures. We're sure to have fun!
But first, say hello and meet my friends...
I'm Muffin the Mule and I love helping my friends. I also love carrots and dressing up! Sometimes I need my thinking cap to get a job done or a problem solved.
MUFFIN

PEREGRINE

Peregrine the Penguin is the brainiest chap I know.
He has a book on anything you want to know – and some things you don't!

MONTY

Monty the Monkey is always up to tricks.
But he never gets into trouble – he swings away through the trees!

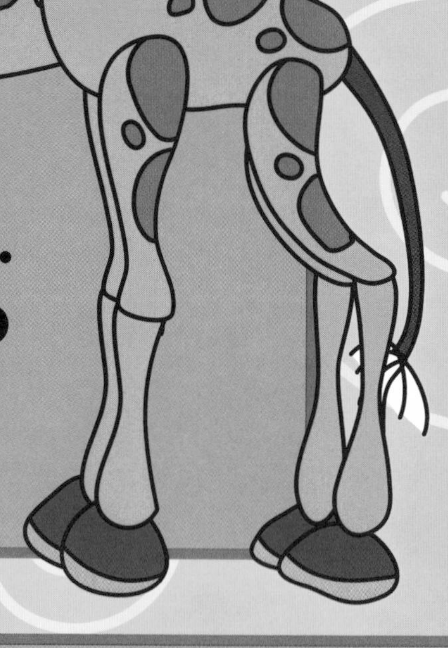

Grace the Giraffe is a girl who likes to gossip. Being so tall, she can't help looking down her nose at people!

LOUISE

Louise the Lamb is as soft and pretty as a woolly jumper! And, luckily for Grace, she likes to gossip too!

Oswald the Ostrich is often in a muddle, but no-one ever gets the better of him – thanks to his clever friend, Willie.

OSWALD

Willie the Worm is the smartest worm you're likely to meet. With Willie's brains and Oswald's legs, there's no stopping them!

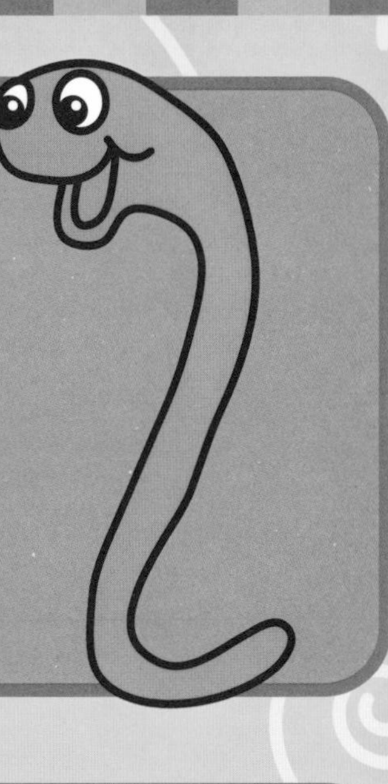

DORIS

Morris and Doris Mouse simply can't do anything without each other – except argue!

Peter the Pup is a friend to everyone. With a 'Sniff!' and a 'Ruff!' he's always ready to help out.

And now you've met everyone in Muffinham, come and see where we all live...

Muffinham is a very special place to live. Shall I show you around? You can find your way on the map.

Let's start at my caravan. It has a red roof and blue steps leading up to the door.

Now, through the open gate and along the path, you come to a house made entirely from wool! Of course, it belongs to Louise the Lamb. It's pink and fluffy and suits Louise to a T!

Carry on through Louise's garden, turn right, and right again, and you arrive at The Sandpit. Now who do you think lives here? (Here's a clue: he likes to bury his head in the sand.) Yes, it's Oswald the Ostrich, and, wherever Oswald is, there you'll find his best friend, Willie.

From The Sandpit there's a path that leads to the coolest house in town. It's round, it's made from ice and it has its own swimming pool! Of course it's Peregrine's igloo.

At the bottom of Peregrine's garden is a lovely old tree. High in its branches is a wooden house. Can you see? The owner of this house loves swinging to his front door! It's Monty's tree house, of course.

Monty's neighbours live behind their own skirting board! Now what kind of creature lives behind a skirting board? Yes! Doris and Morris Mouse!

Through their back garden is a path leading to a kennel. This is where Peter the Pup lives.

Now, follow the path and you're back at my cosy caravan. Which just leaves one building we haven't visited. Can you see? It's out on the edge of the cliffs. It's tall and straight. Someone tall and straight lives here. It's Grace, the giraffe and from her lighthouse she really does have the best views in town!

Which house would you like to live in?

Who's who?

Now you've met all my friends – can you remember where they live? Draw lines to match them to their homes. I've done MYSELF to start you off!

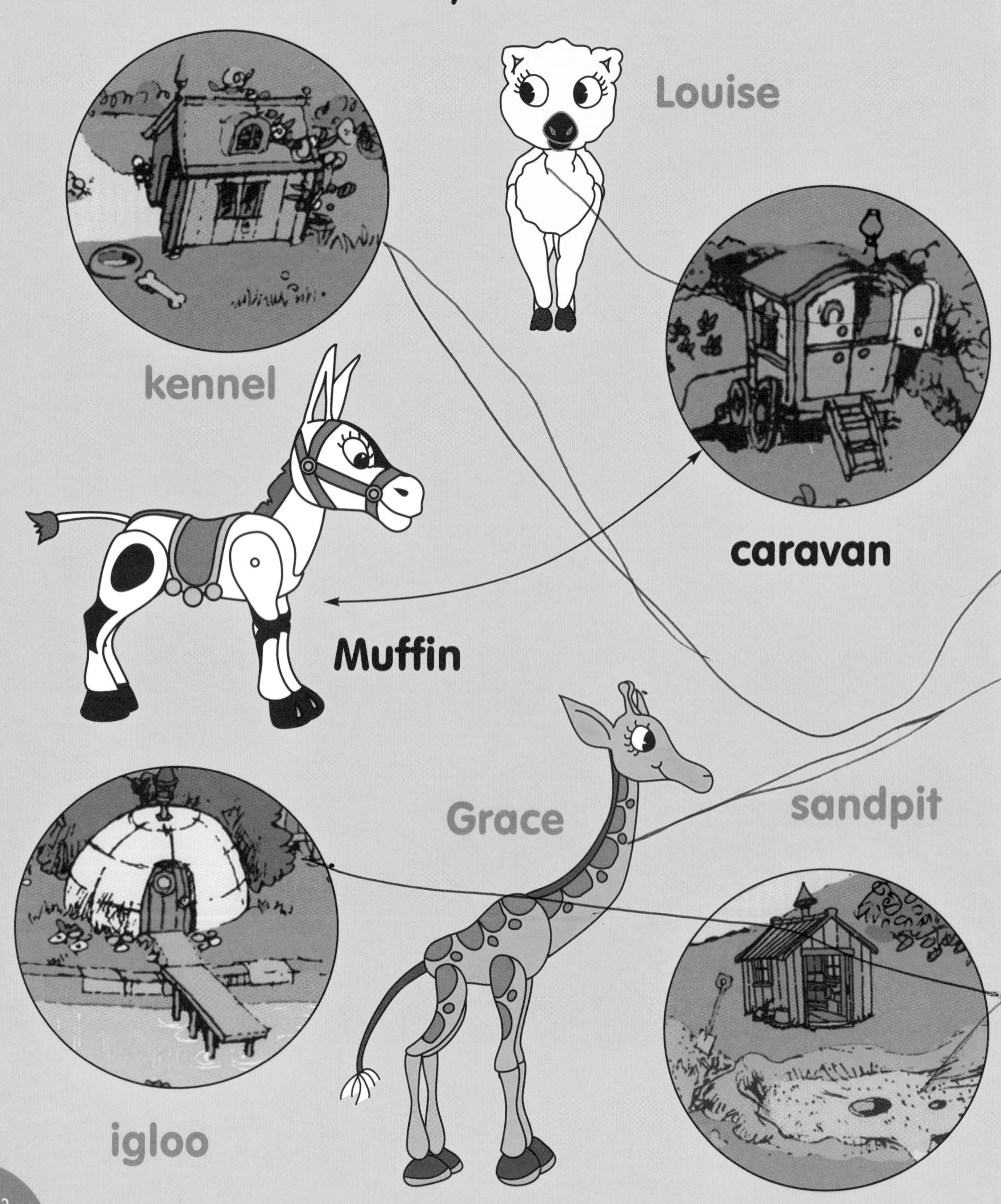

skirting board
Peter
lighthouse
Oswald
and Willie
Monty
Morris and Doris
wool house
Peregrine
tree house

Hello you!

Now you know all about me and my friends, I'd love to know all about you!

Can you write your name and show me what you look like and where you live?

My name is:

....

My best friends are:

....

....

....

This is what I look like:

Stick in a photo or do the drawings yourself!

This is where I live:

Muffin's Day Off

It was a lovely day in Muffinham, and, inside his caravan, Muffin was packing for a picnic.

Into his handkerchief he put...

one carrot cake,

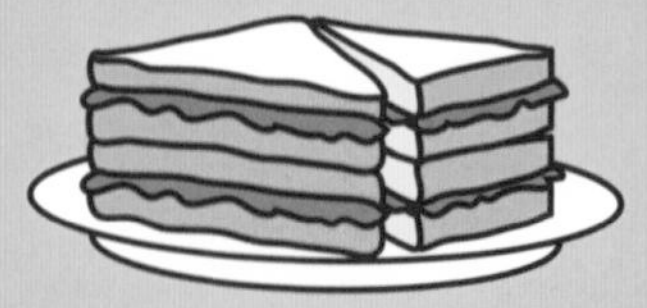

four cress sandwiches,

four juicy apples, two red and two green,

one bottle of elderflower cordial and...

Peregrine's glasses!

"That's not right," said Muffin. "They don't belong!" And he left those on the table.

"But a picnic wouldn't be a picnic without some fresh, crunchy carrots! One, two, three!"

Now the picnic was packed, and Muffin noticed his thinking cap, hanging by the door.

"I won't be needing that!" he said. "Today is my day off!"

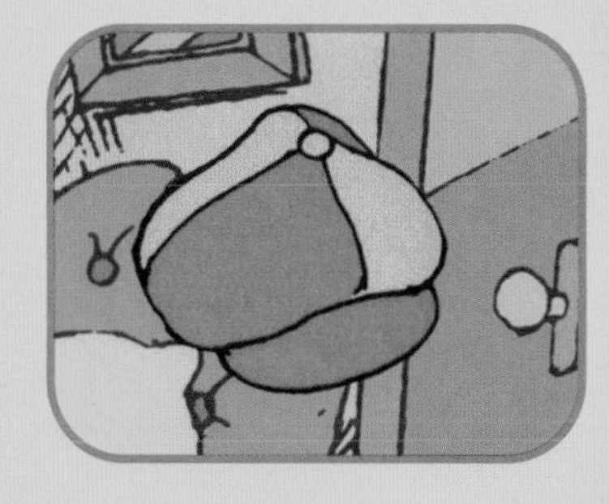

Out in the woods it was a lovely day, too.

"Just the day for swinging in the trees!" sang Monty the Monkey. Until... he screeched to a halt. "Water!" he wailed. "WET water! Help! I'm stuck!"

Luckily, Oswald and Willie were passing by.

"Hey, Monty, what's the matter?" asked Oswald.

"The water's in my way!" cried Monty. "I can't get across!"

"Oh dear..." Oswald was baffled.

"I think we'd better ask Muffin," said Willie, sensibly. "Muffin will know what to do."

Elsewhere in the woods, it was just the day for a gossip. It was getting juicy when...

"My feet!" screeched Grace. "They've turned purple!"

Louise stood and stared. "We'll have to find Muffin," she said. "Muffin will know what to do."

"NOT with purple feet," shrieked Grace, hiding behind a bush.

"All right," sighed Louise, "I'll go and ask Muffin for you." And off she went.

On the way, she passed Peregrine's house. "Do you by any chance have a book on How to Help Giraffes with Purple Feet?" she asked.

"I'm... I'm not sure," said Peregrine. "You see I lost my reading glasses and without my reading glasses, I'm... well, lost!"

"Then come with me to see Muffin," said Louise. "Muffin will know what to do."

At the same time, in another part of town, it was just the day for... an argument!

"Red!" said Morris.
"Red!" said Morris.

"Pink!" said Doris.
"Pink!" said Doris.

Luckily, Peter the Pup was close by.

"What do YOU think, Peter?" said Morris. "Should we have red roses by the front door, or pink?"

Peter had a brainwave. "Er... ruff! Let's ask Muffin!" And off they went to find Muffin too.

Meanwhile, Muffin had laid out his picnic and was feeling completely... bored!

"What's the point of having a yummy picnic on a lovely day without any friends to share it?" he sighed. Then he heard a cry. "Muffin to the rescue!" he called, jumping to his feet. He raced to the stream where he found Monty, stranded.

"Oh, Muffin! How can I cross the stream without getting my feet wet?" cried Monty.

"Well," said Muffin, "you can't go round it...

you can't go through it...

you can't go under it...

but you can go over it."

And, in the blink of an eye, Muffin built a bridge and Monty skipped to safety.

"You're so clever Muffin," said Monty, giving him a hug.

"Come and share my picnic," smiled Muffin.

Meanwhile...

Doris, Morris, Peregrine, Oswald, Willie,

Louise, and Peter,

all arrived at Muffin's caravan.

"Muffin! Ruff, ruff!" called Peter.

"Where can he be?" mused Peregrine.

"He can't be far away," said Louise. "Here's his thinking cap!" She held it up for all to see.

That gave Peregrine an idea. "You're a dog, Peter. You can track Muffin down!"

Peter looked blank.

"Here, take a big sniff."

"Sniiiiiiifffffff!"

"Now, follow that smell!"

At Muffin's picnic, Monty was about to tuck into a huge slice of carrot cake, when a strange sound emerged from a nearby bush.

"Somebody's crying!" Muffin jumped to his feet and raced to help.

"Bother!" said Monty, leaving his cake behind.

Muffin and Monty stared in wonder at the sight of Grace the Giraffe's bright purple feet!

"Cool!" laughed Monty. "I've never seen a Giraffe with purple feet!"

"It's not funny," said Grace, sobbing even louder.

"Now, Grace, tell me when your feet changed colour," Muffin asked, calmly.

"When I was walking through the woods with Louise," she sniffed.

And with that, Muffin bent down and gave her feet a big lick!

"What ARE you doing?" she cried.

"Licking the blackberry juice off your feet!" laughed Muffin. "You must have walked through a patch of blackberries – that's what stained your feet!"

"Oh, Muffin, what would I do without you?"

And all three friends went to enjoy the picnic.

Meanwhile...

Doris, Morris, Peregrine, Oswald, Willie and Louise, were all following Peter, who was following his nose!

And do you know, Peter's nose led them all the way to...

Muffin!

Who soon got to the bottom of things.

"Doris should have pink roses by the front door..." he said, "and Morris should have red roses by the back door!"

They both smiled.

Muffin turned to Peregrine. "Your glasses are on the table in my caravan, exactly where you left them!"

Peregrine smiled too.

"I built a bridge across the water for Monty, and solved the mystery of Grace's purple feet. Now is that everything?"

"Yes, thank you Muffin," they all said.

Then everyone tucked into carrot cake, and cress sandwiches, juicy apples and crunchy carrots with sips of elderflower cordial... and agreed it was the best picnic ever.

"Today really was a lovely day," smiled Muffin, "because I solved all your problems without putting my thinking cap on!"

"Hooray!"

Time for Fun!

"Here's everything I need for my picnic!"

Can you count the things Muffin is packing in his picnic handkerchief? Write your answers in the boxes.

Carrots		**Carrot cake**	
Cress sandwiches		**Green Apples**	
Cordial		**Red Apples**	

Muffin has started his picnic alone.

Which things start with the letter C?
Draw a circle around something that doesn't belong in Muffin's picnic.

Answer: carrots, cake, cordial and cress sandwiches!

"Without my glasses, I'm lost!"

Peregrine is always losing his glasses!
How many pairs can you find hidden inside his igloo?

Answer: 6

"It's Monkey Business!"

Can you finish drawing Monty's face?

"It's just the day for swinging in the trees!"

Copy colour the picture of Monty swinging through the trees.

“My feet have turned purple!”

The blackberry juice made Grace’s feet turn purple. What colour would her feet be if she walked on these fruits? Colour them in using your crayons.

"It's just the day for a gossip!"

Copy colour the picture of Monty, Grace and Louise.

Here are some more trails for Peter to follow. But which one leads to Muffin?

Answer: b.

"Ruufff!"

Can you find the odd Peter out?

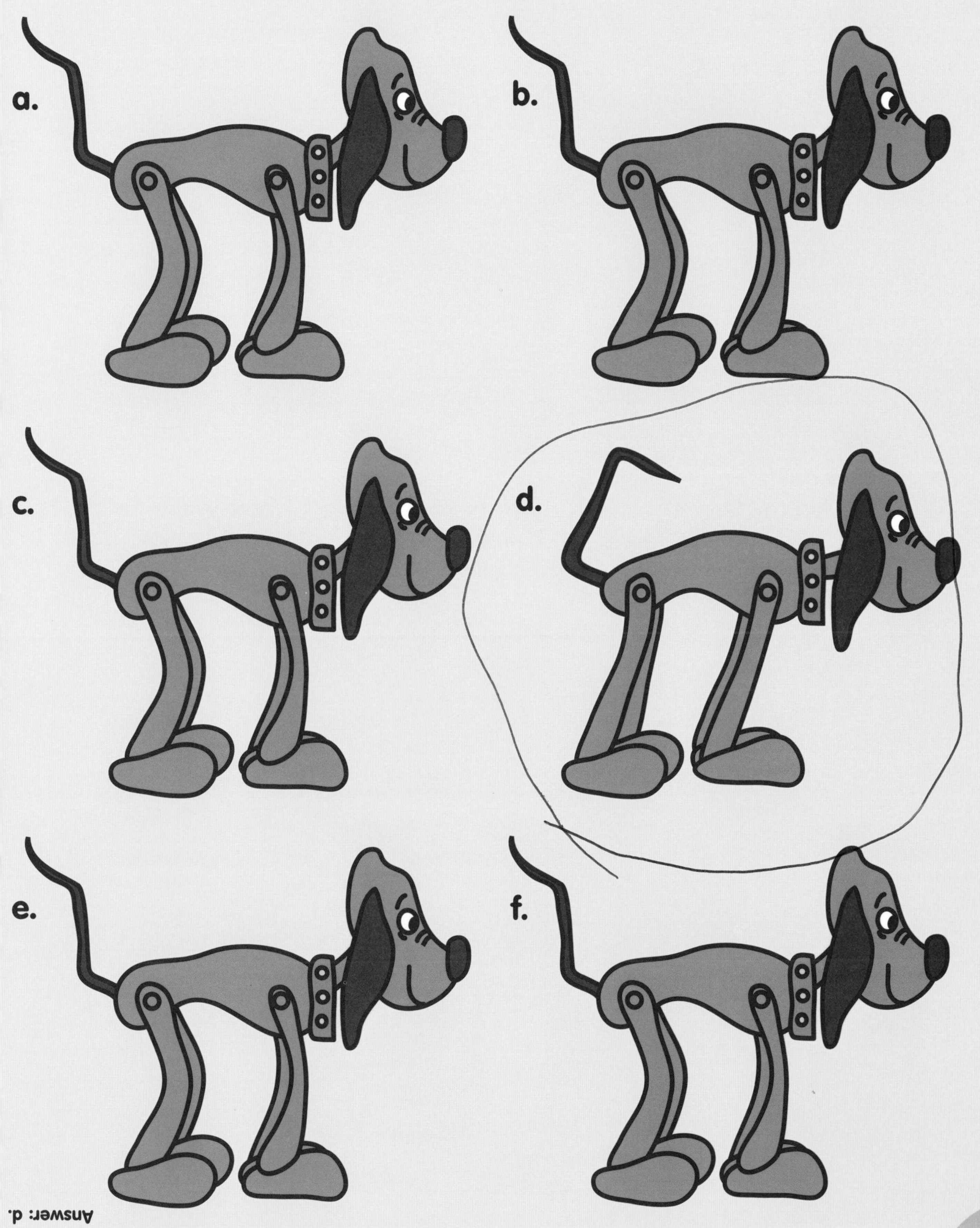

Answer: d.

Peregrine Helps Out

It was early morning in Muffinham and Grace the Giraffe was cross.

"If you don't mind," she said to the seagull who was making a nest on her roof, "this is MY house and you've just woken me up. Now clear off!"

"Awwwk!" said the seagull and put another twig in the nest.

Peregrine was just sitting down to his breakfast when Grace rushed by.

"Good morning Grace," he called.

"Not if you've got a whopping great bird nesting on your house!" she replied.

"Can I help?" asked Peregrine.

But Grace stormed on. "Can't stop – I'm off to ask Muffin what to do."

Grace arrived at Muffin's caravan to find Louise already there.

"I've promised to help Louise with her broken drainpipe," said Muffin.
"But I have a problem," moaned Grace.
"Well, Louise was here first," said Muffin, and he went inside to find his thinking cap.

But that morning in Muffinham, there were more problems to come... Morris and Doris woke to find their water butt had sprung a leak.

And Oswald the Ostrich accidentally sat on his good friend Willie, and then ran off leaving poor Willie behind.

Willie called after his long-legged friend, but it was no use. “If only I wasn’t such a slow coach,” sighed Willie. Then he had an idea. “Maybe Muffin can help! Maybe he can make me go faster!” And off he went, slowly.

By now, just about everyone in Muffinham needed Muffin's help. But poor Willie was the slowest and he only got as far as Peregrine's house.

"What brings you here, Willie?" asked Peregrine.

"I'm on my way to see Muffin," wheezed Willie. "There's something I want him to do for me."

"It's always Muffin," grumbled Peregrine. "Why doesn't anyone ask for MY help? I do have a brain, you know. A rather large and powerful brain, actually!"

"Well, OK," said Willie. "You see... I'm a bit slow. I score a big zero in the leg department. So I was wondering if someone could make me go a bit faster?"

Peregrine stood up straight. "Nothing, my dear worm, could be simpler!" And he was at his drawing board in a flash.

All too soon, a rather impressive vehicle began to take shape...

Meanwhile, Muffin was still trying to mend Louise's broken drainpipe. But it wasn't easy.

"Come on, thinking cap, do your stuff," urged Muffin.

It took so long, that Grace decided to go home to try to scare the seagull away herself.

At the igloo, things were moving much more speedily!

"Da-dah!" announced Peregrine in super-quick time. "Your very own worm-mobile! Climb aboard and let's see what she can do!"

Willie climbed in. Peregrine pressed the large red starter button and Willie and his worm-mobile rocketed into the air!

Heading skywards...

"Watch me go!" whooped Willie. Faster and faster he went...
Until...

"How do you stop it?" he cried, in a trembling voice.

Peregrine looked worried.

"Ah, brakes. I knew there was something I'd forgotten..."

"Help!" called Willie. "DO something!"

And, while Peregrine pondered, Willie became the first ever worm to loop the loop...

the first ever worm to single-handedly remove the seagull from Grace's roof and rehome it in a nearby tree...

the first ever worm to repair the broken drainpipe on Louise's house...

and the first ever worm to crash-land in Doris and Morris's water butt, leaving the nose of the worm-mobile to fill the bunghole perfectly!

Now, Grace and Louise and Morris and Doris were amazed. They were all delighted when Muffin appeared.

"Thank-you for our new bung," said Morris and Doris.
"Thank-you for mending my drainpipe," said Louise.
"Thank-you for shooing away that silly seagull," said Grace.

But before Muffin could speak, Willie emerged from the wreckage.

"It wasn't Muffin," he spluttered. "It was Peregrine!"

"Peregrine?" Everyone turned just as the hero himself arrived.

"Willie!" he beamed. "Thank goodness you're safe!"

"Can someone explain?" asked Muffin.

"Well," said Willie, "Peregrine made me a worm-mobile, and that was what sorted out everyone's problems."

"Well done, Peregrine," smiled Muffin.

"Not really," said Peregrine. "I only wanted to sort out Willie's problem – and I failed."

"No you didn't," said Willie. "From now on I'm quite happy to go at my own speed! In fact, I never want to go fast, ever again!"

Time for Fun!

Morris and Doris are about to have afternoon tea.

Can you find 5 differences in the bottom picture?

Answer: extra jar of sweets on fireplace, cushion changed colour, tea has been drunk in the teacup, label is missing from jam jar and one apple is green in the basket.

All these water butts have lost their bungs!

Can you match the shapes of the bungs to the shape of the holes? Do you know what each shape is called?

"Muffin is my hero!"

Can you finish drawing Muffin's biggest fan?

"I do have a very large brain, you know!"

Join the dots to find out who is visiting Muffin.

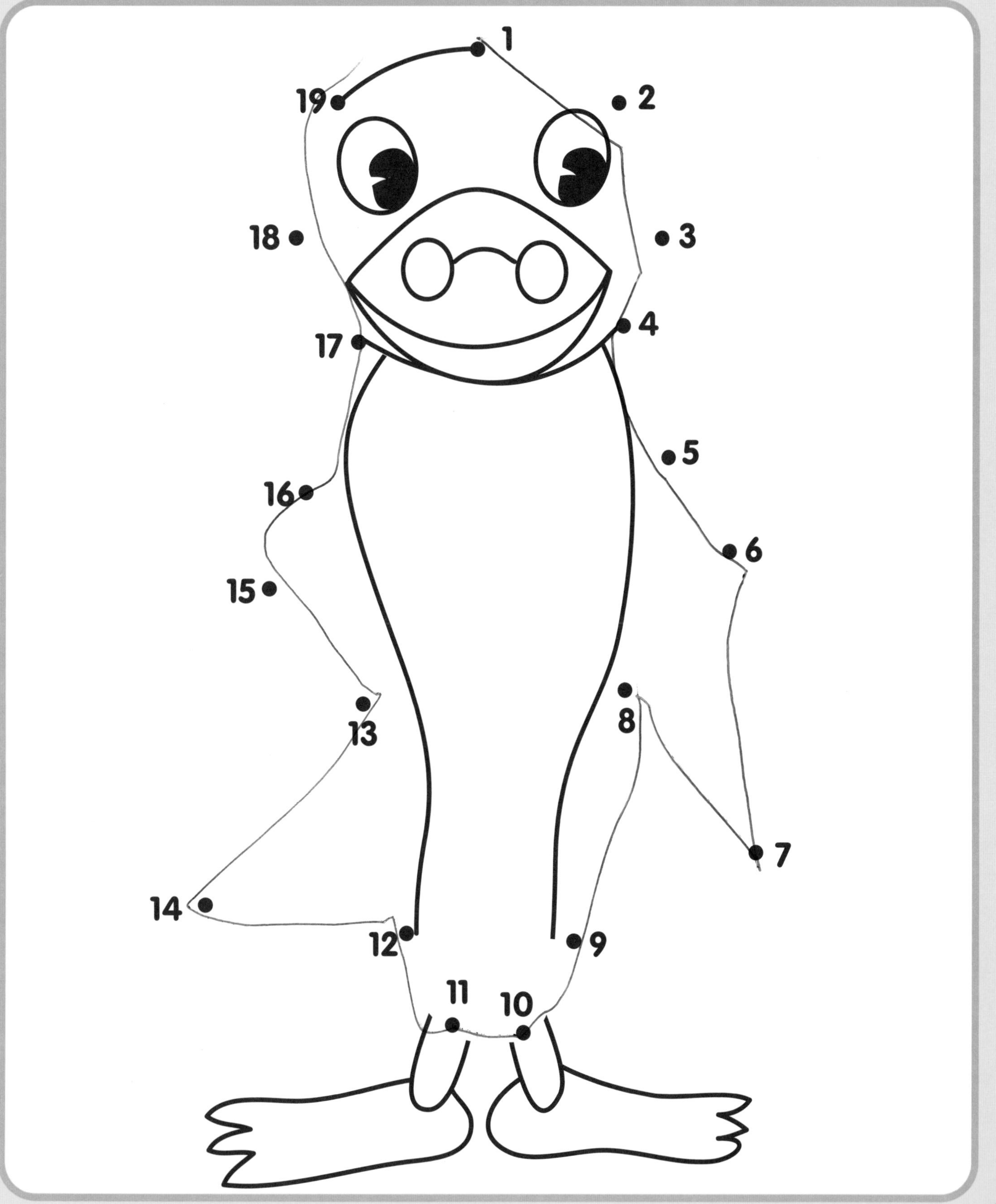

“Look out, here I come!”

Can you find two Montys exactly the same?

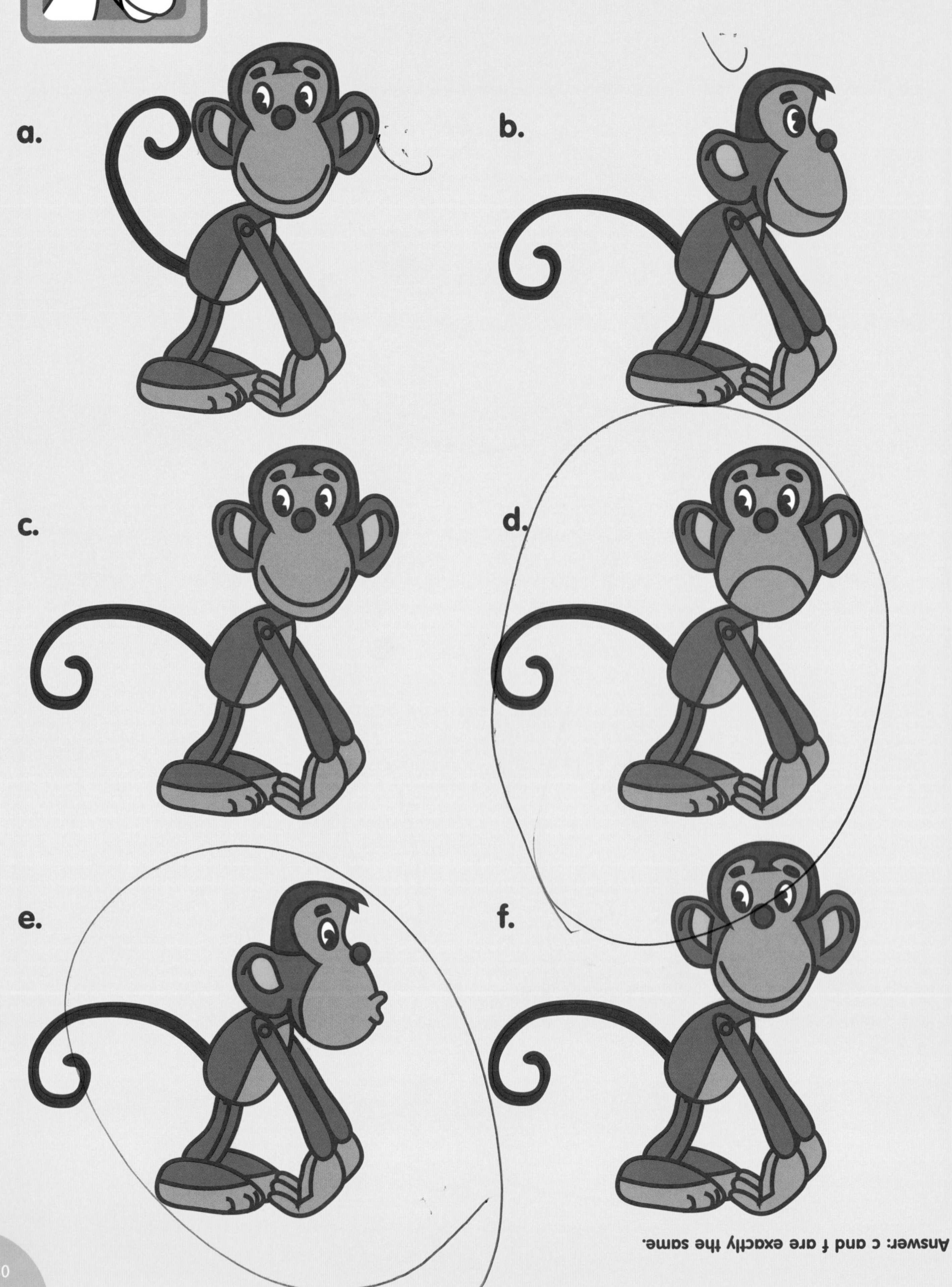

Answer: c and f are exactly the same.

Monty is a messy monkey!

Can you spot five differences between these two pictures?

Answer: porthole window is open, extra bar on electric fire, green apple in fruit bowl, towel has changed colour on trunk and new box has appeared at foot of ladder.

Oswald and Willie's race.

Oswald has long legs and is very fast but Willie the Worm is very slow. Try this colouring race with a friend and see who is fast like Oswald and who is slow like Willie!

How to play:

You will need some crayons, a dice and a friend to play with. Youngest player goes first. Roll the dice and look at the number you have thrown - that's how many sections you can colour on Oswald and Willie. First to colour all their sections wins!

Oswald's Garden Party

Oswald was excited.
"I'm having a garden party,"
he said to Willie and Peter.
"And I'm going to grow all
the food, myself!"

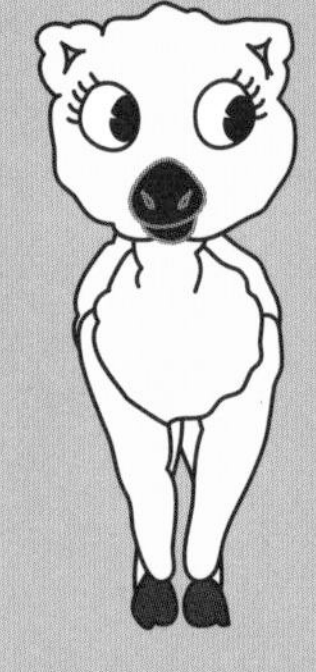

"Raspberries for Louise,
strawberries for Grace,
new potatoes for Morris,
cherry tomatoes for Doris,
iceberg lettuce for Peregrine,
celery for Monty,
carrots for Muffin,
radishes for Willie
and leeks for me!"

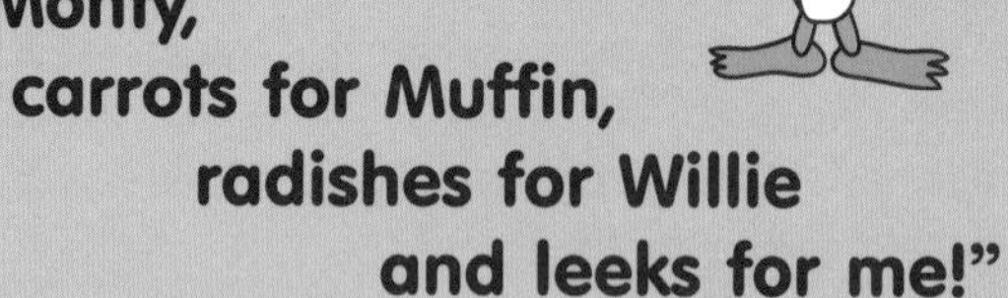

"What about you,
Peter, what can I grow
for you?"

"Ruff! Bones!"
said Peter.

"I can't grow
bones, Peter!" chuckled
Oswald. "But you can
bury some! Come on!"

The three friends set to work in Oswald's garden.

"Ruff! I love digging holes!" said Peter.

"Dig a few more over here!" said Oswald, and he sprinkled seeds into the holes and trampled them in with his very large feet!

A few weeks later, Grace the Giraffe was passing Oswald's garden. Oswald and Willie were on their knees, looking worried.

"Darlings!" she cried, peering over the wall, "has something dreadful happened to my strawberries?"

"It's not your strawberries," said Oswald. "It's Peregrine's lettuces. They've been eaten... by slugs!"

"Let's try shooing them away," suggested Willie.

"Good idea!" agreed Oswald. "Shoo... shoo... shoo..."

They shooed and they shooed, and before long the moon came out and poor Oswald and Willie fell asleep in the lettuce patch.

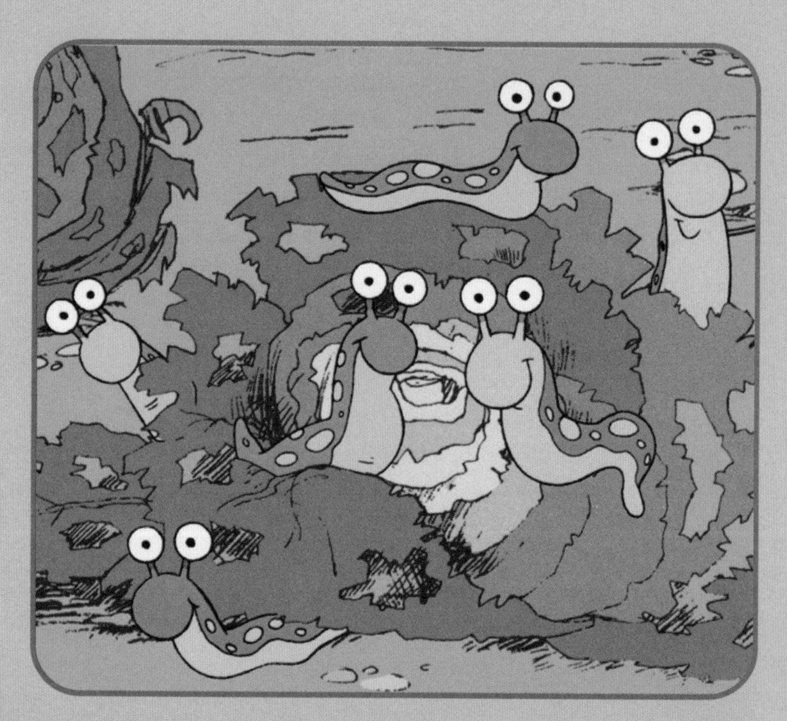

But, next morning, all the slugs had gone!

"They didn't like us sleeping here!" cheered Oswald. Then, he noticed the new potatoes.

"Oh dear," sighed Oswald. "Just look at Morris's new potatoes." Willie looked.

"They're so... small!"

"New potatoes are small!" laughed Willie.

"And they're green!" added Oswald.

"Hmmmm..." thought Willie. "Let's ask Morris if he minds having small, green potatoes."

Morris and Doris were outside their house behind the skirting board.

"I'm worried about your new potatoes," said Oswald, coming into the garden. "They're small... and green."

"Compost is what you need," said Morris, wisely. "Compost makes things grow."

"Where can we buy compost?" asked Willie.

"You don't buy it, Willie, you make it!"

"Oh?" Oswald looked blank.

Doris explained. "You collect together all your garden rubbish in a big heap and leave it in the sun and rain to rot down."

"We can do that!" smiled Oswald. And off they went.

Next day, in the garden, Oswald had collected a very large heap of rubbish. “Now, I’m going to sprinkle it over my plants,” he said, proudly.

“You can’t sprinkle that!” laughed Willie. “It’s too... hard! Let’s go and ask Muffin how to make soft compost!”

Muffin put on his thinking cap. “Hmmm, let me see... how to make soft compost... no, sorry Oswald, nothing comes to mind. But I’m sure Peregrine will have a book on compost heaps!”

So they went straight to Peregrine’s igloo.

Peregrine did indeed have a very large book on gardening. He read out loud: “To make compost, add hungry worms to your garden waste and leave to rot down.”

“Worms!” exclaimed Oswald. “But I don’t have any worms!”

“Willie’s a worm,” said Muffin.

Oswald was shocked. “Willie’s my friend!”

Later that day, Peter and Willie set to work replanting some of the carrots Oswald had flattened with his big feet.

“What are you doing?” scolded Oswald. “I’m in charge of the garden!”

“We were only trying to help,” said Willie.

Willie went and sat by Oswald's compost heap. He didn't like being shouted at.

Suddenly a friendly face popped out.

"Hello," said Willie. "I didn't know there were worms in here." And with that, lots and lots of worms appeared.

"Worms and compost go together like fish and chips," said the first worm.

"Strawberries and cream," said the second worm.

"Burger in a bun," said the third worm. "Worms love compost! Yum, yum, yum!"

And do you know what happened then? Willie dived in!

A few days later, Oswald was frantic with worry.

"Whatever's the matter?" asked Muffin.

"I can't find Willie. I got cross with him and now he's disappeared. I don't know what to do without Willie!"

"Don't worry, Oswald," said Muffin. "We'll find him."

They went to see Peregrine, who found a book all about worms. "Mmm," he said, studying the book. "I never knew worms were so clever! It says here, they make compost heaps go soft by eating the rubbish and passing it through their bodies!"

"Yuk!" said Oswald.

"That's it!" said Muffin. "I know exactly where Willie is!"

Oswald took a deep breath. "Williieeee!" he called, burying his head in the compost heap.

Up popped Willie and tapped him on the shoulder!

"Oh, Willie. I'm so sorry I shouted at you," said Oswald.

"Don't worry," smiled Willie, "I've been having fun in the compost with my friends!"

"And now it's all soft!" grinned Oswald. "You and your worm friends did that, Willie. I don't know what I'd do without you!"

Everyone helped to spread the soft compost on the garden and, a few weeks later...

The raspberries were scrumptious,
the tomatoes tremendous,
the carrots were crunchy,
the celery was heavenly,
the lettuces crisp,
the radishes ravishing,
the leeks were a treat,
the strawberries sweet
and the new potatoes could win prizes!

"Well done Oswald!" everyone said.

"Thank you," said Oswald, "but gardening is a team effort. I couldn't have done it without Willie and his friends!"

"Chomp... chomp... chomp..."

“It’s time for us to go now, see you again next year for more adventures and fun!”

Copy colour Muffin and all his friends.

Contents

A Broadcasting Diamond 1946-2006

Grandmas, Grandads, Mums and Dads are sure to remember watching Muffin the Mule on TV. He is claimed to be the first ever TV star made by the BBC and next year is his 60th birthday!

Not that he looks old! In fact, he looks younger than ever. Muffin is back on our TV screens in a brand new animation series for the BBC - Muffin's first home.

Muffin the Mule was a hugely successful character in the 1950s and 60s and is now very much part of English broadcasting heritage. The TV series is the first new material on the character since the original black and white footage.

It is Muffin's 60th birthday in 2006, so this is a tribute to a character who played a major role in the beginning of children's television programmes. In the 21st century, Muffin will be an animated character who helps others solve their problems.

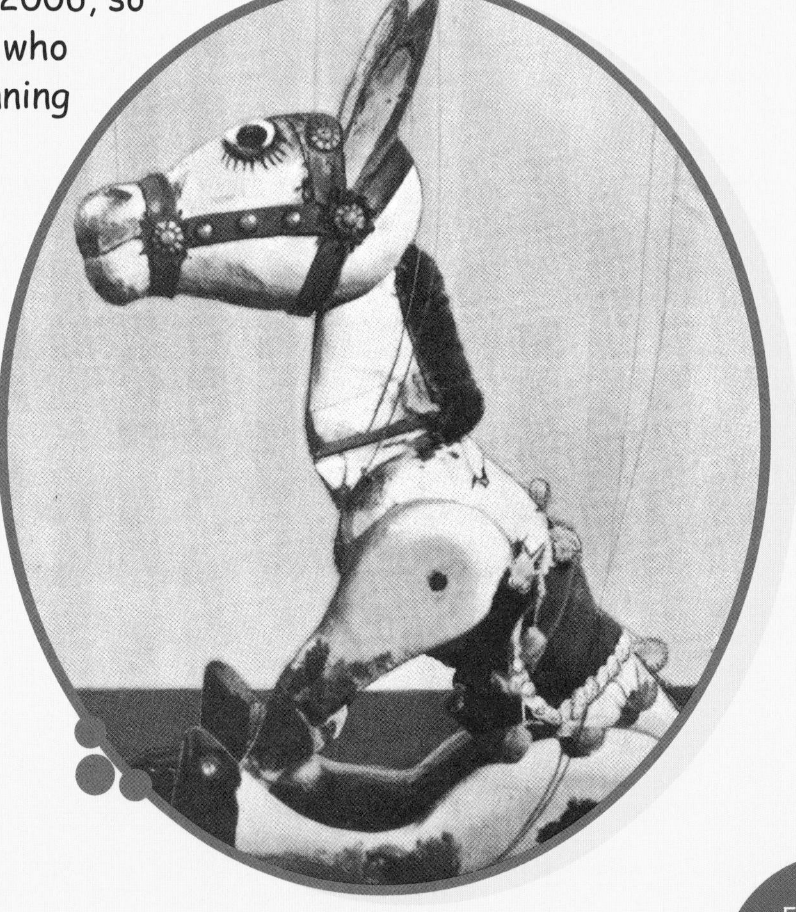

So Muffin the Mule is now entertaining a whole new generation of viewers, but in this, his 60th year, we can look back and remember how it all began...

A Little History ...

Muffin the Mule began life in 1933 as an unnamed character in the Hogarth Puppets puppet circus, run by Jan Bussell and his wife, Ann Hogarth. He was simply known as the "Kicking Mule".

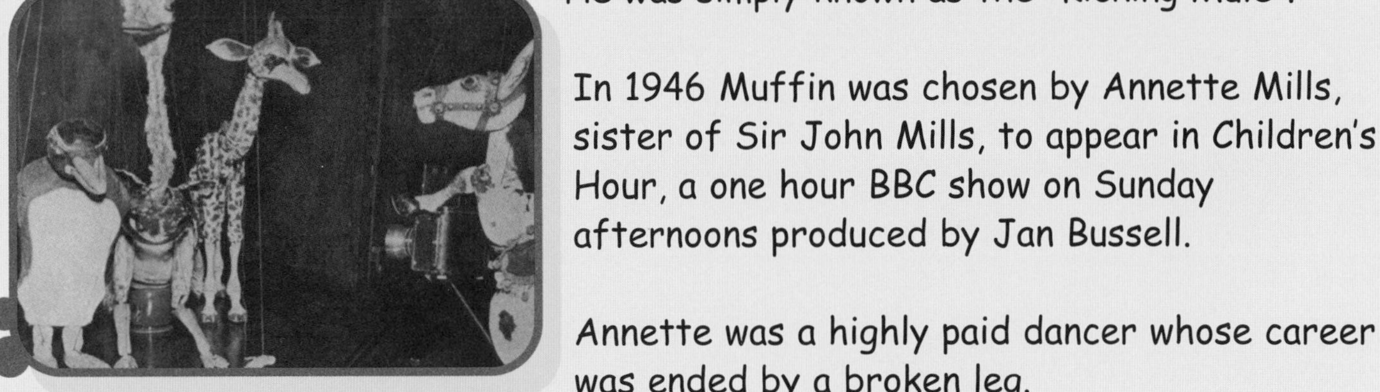

In 1946 Muffin was chosen by Annette Mills, sister of Sir John Mills, to appear in Children's Hour, a one hour BBC show on Sunday afternoons produced by Jan Bussell.

Annette was a highly paid dancer whose career was ended by a broken leg. She joined the BBC in 1946, telling stories and singing songs for children. Noticing one day how the top of her grand piano resembled a stage, she hit upon the idea of populating it with the characters in her stories.

She visited the Hogarth puppets and chose the circus mule, whom she christened 'Muffin'. He made his TV debut on October 20th.

Ann Hogarth wrote the 12 minute scripts and Annette Mills wrote the songs, including the theme tune, 'We want Muffin!' The show became an instant success and the BBC claimed Muffin as 'the first ever star to be made by British Television'.

New characters were soon introduced, including Peregrine the Penguin, Louise the Lamb, Oswald the Ostrich and Willie the Worm.

Muffin's final BBC appearance with Annette Mills was in 1955, just days before she died, aged 61. Muffin continued his TV career on ITV between February and August 1956 in a weekly show which was presented by Jan Bussell and then by his daughter Sally (when she was only 20!) When this series ended, Muffin returned to theatre life with the Hogarth puppets.

Since Ann Hogarth's death in 1994, the original Muffin the Mule puppet has been living with the family of her daughter, Sally McNally (née Bussell) in Devon. He makes the occasional public appearance, but spends most of his time on display in the McNally's living room.

Go Muffin!

Here comes Muffin,
Muffin the Mule,
Dear old Muffin, playing the fool.
Here comes Muffin, everybody sing,
Here comes Muffin the Mule.

What was it like to watch the original Muffin the Mule?
Quite different from the colourful, sophisticated Muffin we see today!

It has to be remembered that watching characters move and talk on the little black and white screen was an exciting experience in itself! We should also remember that the original Muffin was a wooden puppet who clomped around on top of a piano while Annette played the music and Ann Hogarth stood balanced off-camera to pull his strings!

This meant that Muffin couldn't go far, and his storylines were rather limited!!

The stories themselves were made up by Ann Hogarth and Annette wrote and sang the songs. Each episode lasted 12 minutes and was performed live. It would begin with Annette seated at the piano singing the theme tune. The storyline would involve Muffin and many of his other puppet friends – a bossy penguin called Mr. Peregrine Esquire, Grace the Giraffe, Zebbie the Zebra, and Hubert the Hippo, and invariably include a few simple props and some quick changes for the puppets!

To be honest, there was not a great deal of action in Muffin's adventures, due to the obvious limitations of puppeteer and piano, but kindness and honesty always won through – just as in the Muffin stories today.

And each episode ended with a cheery, "Goodbye, 'til next time."

Turn over to read what happened in one classic episode...

Father Christmas Muffin

The scene is set with some festive props on top of the piano - a Christmas tree, a cup and saucer and a bowl of jelly. The theme song fades and Muffin makes his entrance.

He heads straight for the jelly.

"Hey, Muffin, now don't get excited!" warns Annette, wiping his face with her handkerchief. Then she turns to the camera. "This is Muffin's Christmas party, you know." And, while she isn't looking, Muffin dives on the jelly again.

"Muffin!" she scolds. "Now, come along!" (She will only allow so much naughtiness!) "He gets very excited over Christmas and birthdays you know!"

Muffin jumps about noisily and Annette tries to keep him calm. "Yes, lovely tree, lovely everything," she says, translating his clattering for our benefit. "Now, what are you going to do first? Oh, I see! It's a dressing up party!"

Muffin rattles.

"Move the jelly? Move the tree?" She does as she is told and Muffin hurries off to get changed.

Meanwhile, Annette places the tree on her windowsill, then, sitting at her piano, she plays a dramatic drum-roll. Muffin reappears - pushed into shot on a home-made sleigh and curiously disguised as Father Christmas.

"My goodness!" says Annette. "It's Father Christmas himself! With his red cloak and his white beard and riding on a sleigh!"

The perfect cue for a song:

Father Muffin Christmas,
Christmas, Christmas,
My cloak is red,
My beard is white,
I am a truly lovely sight.

How do you like my whiskers?
Whiskers, whiskers,
I bet you don't know who I am,
I bet you a pot of carrot jam,
No, I'm not Louise the Lamb,
I'm Father Muffin Christmas!

"Bravo!" claps Annette, as Muffin has danced all through the song. She tells him to show his costume to the others and he jumps back on the sleigh and is pulled off backwards!

Annette then notices something on top of her Christmas tree. "It's a beautiful fairy queen!" she gasps. (It is, in fact, Louise the Lamb, dressed as a fairy!) "Can you fly, fairy? Will you fly onto my piano? Look at her lovely silver crown, her wand and ballet skirt and wings."

Louise whispers to Annette.

"Oh, it's a surprise for Muffin! I see!" And, as a special treat, Louise is allowed a little dab of powder on her nose. (The equivalent of lip-gloss today!)

Now Louise is ready for her song:

Who is the fairy on the Christmas tree?
Louise, Louise, Louise.
In her little ballet shoes,
There she goes,
With her little wand,
And powder on her nose,

One, two, three,
And a flicker of the tail,
Four, five, six,
How merrily she kicks,
We all love the fairy on the Christmas tree,
Fair Louise the Lamb!

"Bravo!" claps Annette and Louise flies off to see Muffin.

Annette plays another drum roll and Father Christmas comes gliding back on his sleigh. But this Father Christmas is very odd!

"Oh!" says Annette. "I seem to know that beak! It's Mr. Peregrine, Esquire! Look at your lovely cloak and beard - you've almost blinded yourself with that beard! Now what do you represent?" she asks. "Father Peregrine Christmas. I was afraid you were going to say that!" And it's time for Peregrine's version of the song:

Father Peregrine Christmas,
Christmas, Christmas,
My cloak is red,
My beard is white,
I am a truly lovely sight,

How do you like my whiskers?
Whiskers, whiskers?
I bet you don't know who I am,
I bet you a pot of sardine jam,
No, I'm not Louise the lamb,
I'm Father Peregrine Christmas!

But there's trouble ahead! Before Peregrine can leave, Muffin reappears and both Father Christmases become very cross! Standing back to back, they refuse to budge.

Annette has to think of a way to sort out the problem of two Father Christmases! "What about an angry duet to get it off your chests?" she suggests.

I am Santa Claus,
No I am Santa Claus,
You can't be Santa Claus,
Because you look so weird,
in that old beard!

I've got a fine red cloak,
No, I've got a find red cloak,
You can't wear that cloak,
Because I am Santa Claus,
No I am Santa Claus!

Sadly, this doesn't work, but Annette has another idea. "Why don't you two get together and form yourselves into a private company? Two Father Christmases are better than one. You can call yourselves Messrs Christmas!"

Muffin and Peregrine like this idea and go off on the sleigh together!

Meanwhile, a third Father Christmas makes an appearance. None other than Oswald the Ostrich, his sleigh pulled by Willie the Worm wearing antlers!

"Oh, Oswald," laughs Annette, you get everything wrong! Father Christmas has a white beard and a red cloak. You have a white cloak and a red beard! You look like an Arabian knight!" She looks at Willie with his stick-on antlers. "But you are the only Father Christmas with your own reindeer! So I suppose you want a song too!"

I'm Father Oswald Christmas,
Christmas, Christmas,
My beard is red,
My cloak is white,
I truly am a lovely sight!

How do you like my antlers?
Antlers, antlers,
Although I'm only Willie the Worm,
My antlers are really nice and firm,
I hope you like my home-made perm,
I'll draw the sleigh on Christmas day,
For Father Oswald Christmas!

Just then, Messrs Christmas come back.

"Now we're in trouble!" says Annette.

Muffin hands her a card saying: MESSRS XMAS INC. This gives her a brain wave. She says, "You two can be Messrs Christmas, and Oswald can be Inc!"

This seems to do the trick and all three jump on the sleigh and she says farewell with a Christmassy song:

The merrier we'll be,
For his friends are our friends,
And our friends are his friends,
The more we are with Muffin,
The merrier we'll be!

"That was a wonderful finish wasn't it?" says Annette, as Muffin reappears. Then she turns to the camera. "We're going to the party now, so we have to say goodbye everyone, 'til next time."

Muffin - The Transformation

So, Muffin, the clumsy wooden puppet, has been transformed into a colourful sophisticated action hero!

But the new series has remained faithful to the values represented by the classic character.

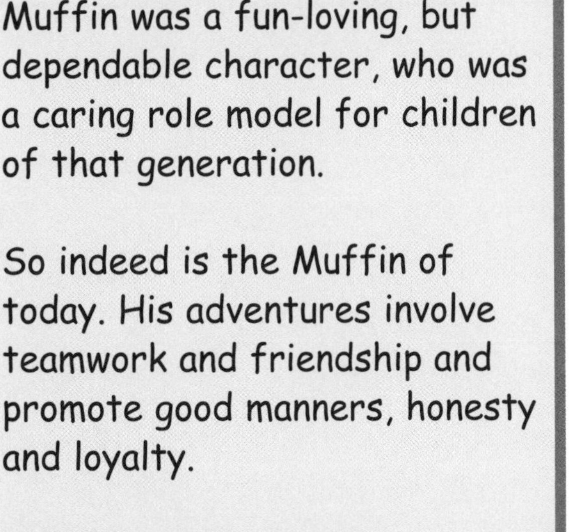

As you will see from the Father Christmas episode, Muffin was a fun-loving, but dependable character, who was a caring role model for children of that generation.

So indeed is the Muffin of today. His adventures involve teamwork and friendship and promote good manners, honesty and loyalty.

Watch any of the new adventures of Muffin and you'll find he's more than happy to help his friends - and there is always a happy ending!

The Muffin the Mule Children's Club

Muffin the Mule©
Collectors' Club
www.Muffin-the-Mule.com
Chairman: Adrienne Hasler Tel: 020 85044943

- Set up in 1999 for collectors of 'Muffinabelia', that is, items produced in the 1950's associated with Muffin and his friends.
- Now includes members whose interest is puppetry or nostalgia TV in general.
- Non Profit making, the Club supports two charities & since 1999, has made donations of over £4000 to them.
- Three newsletters per year & a club afternoon with original puppets in attendance allow members to keep up to date with the latest in Muffin activities.
- **A Muffin the Mule history & vintage memorabilia guide will be out soon.**

If you know a young Muffin the Mule fan who has enjoyed this story, here's your chance to give them another treat.

Simply send their name and your name and address and the new member's birthday (all correspondence will be addressed to the parent or guardian of the new member) and enclose a £1 coin wrapped in the application slip.

We will send them a new, colour, double-sided, Muffin bedroom door hanger and bookmark and very soon afterwards, details of the new Muffin the Mule Children's Club.

They will also receive special offers and the latest Muffin updates in a regular newsletter.

Send us the address details required now (with your £1 coin) to:

Muffin the Mule Children's Club, Maverick Entertainment Ltd,
Belmont House, 13 Upper High Street, Thame, Oxon OX9 3ER
(please allow 28 days for delivery).

Plus

Every applicant has a chance of winning the new *Wish Upon a Star* DVD, featuring Muffin and all his friends. We've got 50 copies to give away. Simply add the answer to the following question to the piece of paper carrying your address details.

"What does Muffin usually put on his head to help solve his friend's problems?"

50 winners will be drawn at random.
Closing date for entries is 27th January 2006.

Good Luck!

Here is a member's badge from the original Muffin Collector's Club which was set up in the 1950s.

Today you can still join the original Muffin Collector's Club online at: www.muffin-the-mule.com

Brand new adventures of Muffin DVD!

A Muffin the Mule Day

Idea and Words by Patrick Talbot
Photographs and layout by Adrienne Hasler

Imagine life about 50 years ago for a school age child lucky enough to watch Muffin at home in front of the 'goggle-box'.

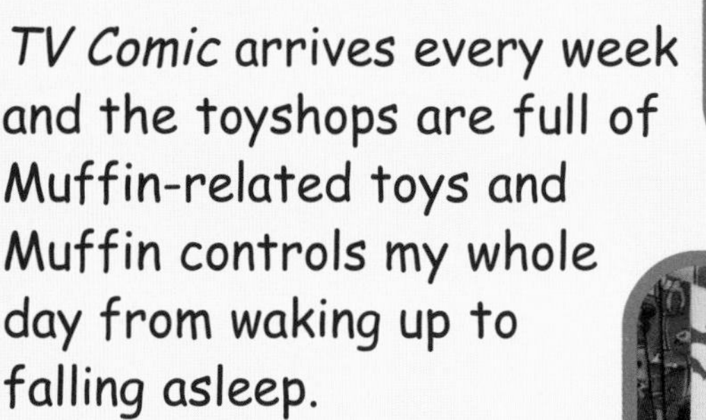

TV Comic arrives every week and the toyshops are full of Muffin-related toys and Muffin controls my whole day from waking up to falling asleep.

Meals, playtime, schoolwork, story-time, children's parties and bedtime are all full of Muffin the Mule and his friends.

A television superstar had been created by Ann Hogarth, Jan Bussell and Annette Mills and the Muffin Syndicate and Muffin Syndicate Limited were determined that every opportunity was taken to remind the children of Britain of their friend Muffin.

Mummy comes into my bedroom at 6.45 am and wakes me up.

The Muffin curtains are pulled open and I step out onto my Muffin rug and into my Muffin slippers.

Into the bathroom for a wash - will it be my Muffin, Louise, Zebbie or Esk & Moe Cullingford's soap?

"Get dressed before breakfast and don't be late for school!"

Put my nightdress into my Muffin pyjama case, turn off my Muffin bedside lamp, put on my Muffin twin set, with my Muffin hanky up my sleeve, tie my hair up with my Muffin ribbon, pin on my Muffin brooch and badge and slide down the banisters to breakfast.

Oh, good! Mummy has put my Muffin napkin ring by my place, with my Muffin knife, fork and spoon and I put on the Muffin badge I bought when I went to see Muffin at Woolacombe Beach on Sunday.

I'm helping Mummy with breakfast wearing my Muffin apron. Breakfast off my Muffin plate and milk out of my Muffin mug, poured from the Muffin jug. (And perhaps a piece of cake?)

Music practice next.

Where's the 'We Want Muffin' music and where's the *First Muffin Songbook* and why don't Chappells bring out a second songbook? I can play 'We Want Muffin' and 'Sally the Seal' now. What shall I learn to play next?

I know. 'Make way for Mr. Peregrine Esquire.'

Off to school at 8.15. Pack my satchel with my Muffin pencils, especially my new Muffin and Peregrine propelling pencils, my Muffin notebook and crayons, and my Muffin drawing slate.

It's needlework today and so I must remember my Muffin Busy Box and Embroidery Set.

Tomorrow it's Art; I must remember to take my Muffin painting book and paintbox and modelling set.

Is there any money in my Muffin moneybox? I do hope so. I walk past the toyshop on the way to and from school and I've been saving up for a Muffin TV set with special films and filmstrips.

After school I play with my Muffin tea set and puppets. The picture cubes are super, aren't they? And Granny sends a Muffin postcard every week!

At the weekend it's my friend's birthday party. He's 7 years old. Let's play Pin the Tail on Muffin, Muffin's Derby Game, Muffin's Skittles and sing along to lots of Muffin songs on the gramophone. Anyone for a hand of Muffin snap?

And after tea it's time for bedtime stories, tonight it's the *Muffin Blue Book*. Oh, one more story! Why not *Muffin's Own Storybook*?

Good Night Children.
Good Night Muffin.

mike@toysteam.com

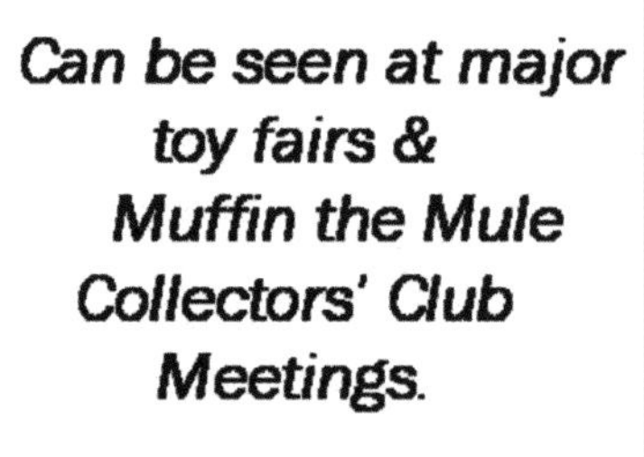

Trading in vintage toys

Can be seen at major toy fairs & Muffin the Mule Collectors' Club Meetings.

Tel/fax: 024 76 415608

Steve Penny - Pure Nostalgia

DEALER IN SECOND HAND CHILDREN'S ANNUALS, BOOKS AND COMICS.
ALSO SCI-FI &
ASSOCIATED COLLECTABLES

Best prices paid for full collections & odd items especially Rupert, Beano, Andersons, Cartoons, Film Annuals & TV related etc.

****

Nearly 20,000 items for sale at any one time.
Please telephone your requirements.
Wants lists welcome.

Tel:01375 402467
www.purenostalgia.co.uk

Muffin the Mule

1946-2006

A History & Collectors Guide

****

Available from 1st September
Price £15.00 + p&p
*Pre Order Price : £13.00 + p&p

This book is the first accurate and comprehensive record of the history of this internationally famous puppet.
It includes original advertising as source references plus previously unpublished photographs, anecdotes and original documentation for the most popular die cast toy, the Moko Muffin Junior

Section one: Muffin and the Hogarth puppets from his television years up to the present day. There are some 34 black and white or colour photographs within this section.
Many never in print before now.

Section two: Recollections by Sally McNally who was the daughter of the original puppeteer, Ann Hogarth.
These are reprinted from the Club newsletters.

Section three: Collectables guide. Approximately 150 photographs illustrating 57 different categories of vintage items
In addition, there is identification of items that are thought to be Muffin (but are not) and a page of 'Collectors' Club only' items.

To order:
Tel:020 8504 4943
Or via the web site:
www.Muffin-the-Mule.com